TALES FROM A JUNIOR GRANDMOTHER

A book of "Bubbe Meises"

CYNTHIA S. GOREN

COVER AND DESIGN BY JACOB A. SHAW

Happy reading!

Cynthia Goren

AuthorHouse™
1663 Liberty Drive
Bloomington, IN 47403
www.authorhouse.com
Phone: 1-800-839-8640

Published by AuthorHouse 07/17/2012

ISBN: 978-1-4772-4096-0 (sc)
*   978-1-4772-4097-7 (e)*

Library of Congress Control Number: 2012912250

Any people depicted in stock imagery provided by Thinkstock are models,
and such images are being used for illustrative purposes only.
Certain stock imagery © Thinkstock.

I dedicate this little book first to my husband, Sy, my love, my best friend, and my cheerleader in all things;

and to my grandchildren, Maeli, Ben, Jacob, Yael, and Maya, whose soaring imaginations have been my constant inspiration.

CONTENTS

PREFACE

What grandmother hasn't thrilled to the delicious nighttime invitation from her grandchild to "tell me a story?" Getting in bed with the child of our child, we wrap ourselves in memories from the past and hopes for the future. When we run out of "ready-made" stories, we invent them, and those prove to be the favorites.

This is one Jewish grandmother's "made-to-order" collection of stories. While they have a decided Jewish "flavor," I hope that the messages are universal. A common theme of all of them involves love—of each other, of family, of peoplehood, and of nature.

As children grow, their need for stories does not ebb, but the stories themselves must "grow" in content. The stories in this book have been placed in order from the whimsical and fantastical for the very young, to those of more serious content for the older child.

The latter two stories, although fiction, were inspired by true-life situations. While there may not actually be a child with David's disability in "Bar Mitzvah for the Birds", there are many children who learn in ways different than most others do. However, with the help, patience, and encouragement of family and professionals, these children can learn. "Caleb, the Oketz Dog" was inspired by an actual incident that occurred in Helena, Montana in 2009. It was a challenge and a great deal of fun to create a story around it.

I have enjoyed my journey from telling tales written by others to creating and sharing my own. More importantly, my grandchildren have enjoyed the journey, as well.

GRANDMA'S FIRST MATZO BALL

Ari loved to go to Poppa and Grandma's house for the holiday celebrations. He loved to smell the sometimes sweet, sometimes spicy aromas that floated through the house. He loved to feel the textures of the different holiday foods on his tongue—sometimes smooth, sometimes crunchy, sometimes hot and sometimes cold. Often the tastes were a little bit different from everyday food and he thought it was fun trying to get used to them.

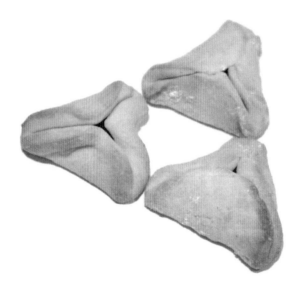

But Ari did not know Grandma's secret. It is a secret that most grandmas have. It is a secret that their children and grandchildren sometimes never learn! Grandma's secret was that she did not always know how to cook those delicious foods! Her secret was the story of her first matzo ball.

It happened a long, long time ago when Grandma was very young. Young means right after Grandma and Poppa were married. Young means before they had any children, when they lived alone, and when Grandma worked as a teacher. And young sometimes means not asking for help.

It was right before Passover, or "Pesach" as everyone in the family called it. It was the first Pesach that Poppa and Grandma would spend together as husband and wife.

Grandma knew the story of Passover. She knew that the Hebrews had been slaves in Egypt and that God had selected Moses to rescue them, to lead them through the desert to the Land of Israel. She knew that the Hebrews, or Israelites as they were also called, had to leave Egypt in a hurry. She knew that they didn't have time to let their dough rise into bread and that, because of their haste, they had to eat unleavened bread, or matzo. She knew that is why we cannot eat bread during the eight days of the holiday. But Grandma was also aware that there were many other foods besides bread that Jews cannot eat during this holiday, especially those foods made with flour that has not first been made from matzo.

Grandma knew that there could be no regular flour noodles for her chicken soup, no rice, no kreplach. Grandma knew that she would have to make matzo balls.

There was only one problem! She didn't know how to make matzo balls! She loved the light, fluffy, rich taste of Great-Grandma Bebe's matzo balls, but she had never asked Bebe how to make them!

"How hard could it be to make such small little things?" Grandma asked herself. "There are not many ingredients in matzo balls, just eggs, matzo meal, oil, water, and salt! I'll just put a little bit of each and surely it will be okay."

Grandma took down her large bowl from the cabinet, her mixing spoon, and her measuring utensils. She took out some eggs from the refrigerator, some matzo meal, salt and oil from the pantry. First she mixed the matzo meal and salt together. Then she put some eggs in the bowl and beat them. Then she put some oil in the eggs and a lot of water. When she finished pouring the matzo meal into the eggs she said, "This doesn't look like a ball—it looks too loose, like applesauce! I think I'll add more matzo meal." But after adding more of it to the mixture Grandma thought, "It still doesn't look like a ball; it looks like oatmeal." So she added more and more matzo meal until Grandma finally said, "Now the matzo meal mixture is a ball; now I will put it into a pot of boiling water and soon I will have a yummy matzo ball!"

Grandma waited until the water in the pot boiled fast and furiously. She gathered up the matzo ball-egg mixture in her hands, smoothed it into a ball and dropped it into the pot.

"Kerplunk!" went the matzo ball as it hit the bottom of the pot. The loud sound frightened her as the pot shivered and shook from the large blow of the matzo ball. **"I didn't know matzo balls were so loud!"** she said.

Grandma remembered that matzo balls were supposed to pop up to the top of the pot as they cooked, so she happily watched the pot, waiting for the ball to spring up and bounce around in the bubbling water.

She watched and watched. She waited and waited. But the matzo ball never got off the bottom of the pot! After a long while Grandma thought, "I think it's time to take this matzo ball out of the pot." First she tried with a spoon, but the matzo ball was too heavy to lift.

Then, pulling as hard as she could, she tried to get it out with a soup ladle, but it was still too heavy.

Then she called out to Poppa, "Sy, would you please get a shovel? This matzo ball is just too big for me to lift! **I didn't know matzo balls were** so **heavy!**"

So Poppa went to the garage to get the garden shovel. He scrubbed it clean and brought it to the kitchen. He lowered the shovel into the pot and *Hurrah!* He was able to get the matzo ball out of the pot.

"Where should I put it?" asked Poppa, straining as he held the heavy shovel with its huge load. Grandma got her largest platter, put it on the counter, and Poppa laid the matzo ball on it. *Crash!* went the platter, as the matzo ball broke it into five pieces. "Oh, my beautiful holiday platter," cried Grandma. "It did not know what hit it! Can you fix it?" she asked Poppa.

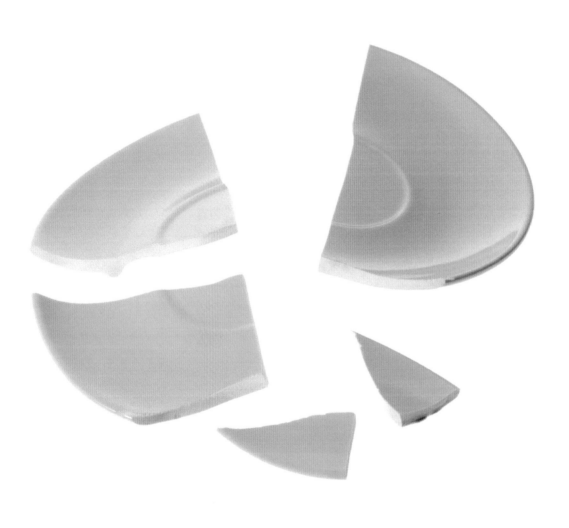

Since Poppa can fix anything, of course he was able to fix Grandma's platter as the matzo ball cooled. Now it was time to cut the "knadle" (that is what Grandma likes to call it).

First Grandma tried to cut it with the side of a spoon. She couldn't.

Then Grandma tried to cut it with a fork and knife. She couldn't.

Then Grandma tried to cut it with a challah knife. She couldn't.

In desperation, Grandma called to Poppa. "You'd better get your saw! **I didn't know that matzo balls were so hard!**"

So Poppa went down to the basement to get his saw. He walked slowly up the stairs saying to himself, "This is some matzo ball."

Poppa was able to cut the matzo ball with the saw, but he had to get a new blade for the saw when he was finished. The matzo ball certainly didn't taste very good, but at least Grandma tried.

From then on whenever Grandma made new holiday foods, she always either asked for a recipe from someone or found a recipe in a cookbook. Many times she would make some changes, but she always started with a recipe.

Grandma's matzo balls, called "knadlach" in Yiddish, are now delicious. They are soft, puffy, yellow, juicy and rich. Grandma puts in just the right amounts of the ingredients. She now knows that in order for the batter to become balls it must first be refrigerated and then cooked. The little balls then bounce around at the top of the pot doing a little circle dance until they are done and ready to be eaten.

Above all, Grandma adds one magic ingredient that all Grandmas use, and that is *Love.* Unlike matzo meal, that is the only ingredient of which you can never use too much.

If you would like to make Grandma's matzo balls, here is her recipe:

1 cup matzo meal
1 teaspoon salt
4 eggs
¼ cup seltzer or club soda
¼ cup vegetable oil

Bring eggs to room temperature. Combine matzo meal and salt in small bowl. Beat eggs in separate larger bowl and add seltzer and oil. Mix well. Add matzo meal to egg mixture and stir thoroughly. Add gallons of **LOVE.** Refrigerate 30-40 minutes. In large pot boil 3 ½ quarts of water with 1½ teaspoons of salt. Form mixture into balls about the size of ping pong balls and drop into boiling salted water. Cook on low heat for 30 -40 minutes or until done. Makes about 10-11 matzo balls. *Don't forget to wet your hands often when forming the batter into balls so that the batter doesn't stick to your hands! And don't lick your hands—raw eggs are not good for you.* Take out finished matzo balls with slotted spoon and cool on large cookie sheet. When cool, put cookie sheets on which matzo balls have been placed into freezer, if desired. When frozen, transfer to plastic bags.

DANNY'S CHANUKAH MIRACLE

Danny awoke from his afternoon nap, looked out his bedroom window and said, "Chanukah is in the air. Snow is everywhere! It is a carpet on the ground, an icing on the trees, and looks like confetti as it slowly tumbles down from the sky. I am excited. I love Chanukah!"

As he continued to peer through the window, he began to think about the story of Chanukah. Although it happened at this time of year many years ago, he knew that in Jerusalem and the country around it, where the story takes place, there would not have been much snow. Poppa and Grandma had told him that when they were in Israel in winter, it had been very warm.

Danny tried to picture what the characters in the Chanukah story would have looked like. He knew that the people did not dress as we do today. He knew that the Greek king, who was named Antiochus, made all the people of his empire, including the Jews, give up their ways of dressing, their customs, and their religions. Everyone had to follow the Greek way of doing things. And Danny knew that this was a big problem for the Jews.

Danny could not imagine having to give up being Jewish. He could not imagine a Friday night without his mother lighting candles, without his father saying the "Kiddush," without a beautiful, shiny, twisted challah on the table. He could not imagine being told that he had to eat pork, or shrimp or to pray in ways other than Jewish ones—to pray to many gods instead of the one God of the Jews.

"How sad it must have been for the Jewish people to watch the Greek soldiers enter the Temple and destroy all the holy objects in it—the Torahs, the prayer books, the beautiful decorations. How they must have cried when the Jewish Temple was made into a Greek Temple!" Danny thought that he would cry if he saw that happen to his synagogue.

"I would fight to keep the Temple Jewish. I would fight to be able to pray to God in the way of my people. I would be like Judah Maccabee," Danny thought. He knew that when Judah's brave father, Mattathias, died, Judah became the leader of all the Jewish soldiers who hid out in the hills, waiting to attack their Greek enemies. Whenever Danny thought of Judah he raised his arm and clenched his fist as if he were carrying a hammer, because Grandma told him that "Maccabee" means "hammer".

As Danny stared out the window, he thought of Judah's army, tired and hungry, sleeping on the hard uncomfortable ground in the mountains around Modin. He knew that although there would not have been much snow, it could be pretty cold at night in the mountains. He could hear Judah talking to his men, encouraging them not to give up. He could hear him say, "I know we can do it. We can get our Temple back. You must help me."

"If I were to have lived then, I would have helped Judah," Danny thought. "I would have been a Maccabee," he said, with his arm in the air, holding an imaginary hammer. "I would have marched to Jerusalem to get our Temple back."

Danny thought of the awful mess he would have found, when, as a Maccabee, he would have entered the Temple that had been ruined by the Greeks. Again he thought how he would he feel if he entered his own synagogue and saw things burnt, broken, filthy and some things even gone! He could not even imagine how sad he would be.

He knew also that, if he were in Jerusalem, he would have helped to clean up the mess. He would have scrubbed where things were dirty, repaired where things were broken, and rebuilt and remade things that had disappeared. He would do just as Judah did—restore the Temple to the beautiful condition it was in before Antiochus' soldiers entered it.

Danny smiled as he thought of the tiny bit of oil that the Maccabees found in the Temple—just enough for the Menorah to burn one day. He giggled as he pictured the look on people's faces as the Menorah burned not one, but eight days! The Chanukah Miracle.

"What a shame that miracles don't happen anymore," Danny thought. "I would love to see a miracle."

Just as he began to think some more about miracles, he heard his mom calling him. "Danny, it's time to go to Grandma and Poppa's house to make potato latkes. You'd better get your jacket, hat, mittens, and boots on. Hurry!"

It was a slow ride to Poppa and Grandma's house because of the weather. In the car, watching the windshield wipers go back and forth as they gathered the snowflakes in their blades, Danny kept thinking about that miracle question. Why hadn't he seen any miracles? Did some people see them? Or, as he thought before, did they just not happen anymore?

When he and his family arrived at his grandparents' home, Danny could not wait to ask Grandma and Poppa his questions. "Why haven't I seen any miracles? Do they still happen? Have you ever seen a miracle?"

Grandma scooped him up in her arms, kissed him, and said, "Of course, there are still miracles, Danny. You are our miracle—a bright little boy, who always has the right questions to ask, who often has his own answers, and whom we love very much."

While Grandma's answer was very nice, Danny was not satisfied. "I want to see a miracle happen, before my eyes," he said.

"Just keep your eyes open," said Grandma, "and you will see a miracle. They still do happen, every day."

Danny wondered when his miracle would happen, but these thoughts would have to wait, because it was time to make the latkes. As he helped Grandma and Poppa peel and cut the potatoes, Danny thought about the Maccabees, hiding out in the hills of Modin, cold and hungry. As he helped to peel and grind the onions, his "onion" tears reminded him of the tears the Jewish people shed when their Temple was vandalized and made impure. When he combined the potatoes, onion, eggs, salt, baking powder, and matzo meal, he thought of all the many people who lived under Antiochus' rule and lost their identity and their specialness as the King commanded them to "mix" and be like everyone else. As he watched Grandma heat up the oil until it began to bubble and spurt, he thought of the small amount of oil, only a day's worth, that miraculously lasted for eight days in the Temple. And Danny waited for his own miracle to happen.

As Grandma and Poppa slowly spooned the potato batter into the hot, bubbly oil, the latkes began to take shape. And what shapes they were! Grandma's first latke looked a little silly; it was long and skinny, with a piece going across its top. "It looks like a hammer," Danny cried. "It looks like Judah's hammer!"

Before he could get over his excitement, Jacob looked at Poppa's pan and saw his first latke. It looked like it had eyes on it, where the darker bits of potatoes had gathered, and soon two things that looked like legs began to form. Then a sword and a shield seemed to add themselves on to the pancake. "Wow, it's Judah Maccabee," exclaimed Danny. "Poppa's latke is Judah Maccabee!"

"And look, Danny, look at my second latke!" said Grandma as she pointed to a pancake with six points on it.

"Grandma, it's a Jewish star; it's a Mogen David. I can't believe what is happening here!" The latkes are all taking special Chanukah shapes. This is truly a miracle!"

Soon latkes that were shaped like dreidels and some like menorahs joined the other latkes in the pans. Even the little dark brown bits of latke pieces that swam around in the oil became, in Danny's mind, the broken remains of the Temple treasures that the Greeks had destroyed.

Now Grandma had enough batter for only one more latke. What shape would this last pancake take? Danny could hardly wait. Poppa, Grandma, and Danny all watched as the batter began to take form. What would it be? It also looked like it had eyes... and then legs... and then... and then... *it was Danny!* Danny was in the pan with Judah, his hammer, the broken treasures, the menorahs, the dreidels—another miracle!

As Grandma gently took each latke out from the pan and laid them on her beautiful platters, she took Danny's hand and spoke to him softly and clearly. "Danny darling, you have seen your own Chanukah miracle. Not only did the latkes take special Chanukah shapes, but *you were in the pan with them.*

"Today as you told yourself the story of Chanukah, you felt as though you were really in Modin and in Jerusalem with Judah Maccabee. You felt everything the Jewish people felt then. You were sad for them when they suffered, and you rejoiced with them when they celebrated. You are part of the Chanukah miracle."

Danny thought a lot about what Grandma said. He loved his Chanukah miracles that took shape in Grandma and Poppa's pans. But he realized that there was a miracle even bigger than they were. The biggest miracle of all is the Jewish people, who live on and on to tell their stories.

If you would like to make Grandma's potato latkes, here is her recipe. It serves many people, so invite the whole family!

7 eggs

1 cup grated onions

½ teaspoon pepper

4 teaspoons salt

2 teaspoons baking powder

1 cup matzo meal

8 lbs. Idaho potatoes peeled and cubed

Grind peeled and cubed potatoes and onions. Press out excess water from potatoes, using a fine colander. Grind onions. Combine potatoes, onion, eggs, salt, baking powder, and matzo meal. Fry in oil. Sit pancakes on paper towels to drain off excess oil. Freeze on cookie sheets, if desired, and then in plastic bags. Reheat frozen at 425' or defrosted at 400'.

A BAR MITZVAH FOR THE BIRDS

For a bird of the skies will carry your voice
And a winged creature may report the word.

Ecclesiastes 10:20

CHAPTER ONE

It was one of those "don't forget" days. "Don't forget to pack your bathing suit." "Don't forget to take a hat." "Don't forget the sunscreen." "Don't forget your binoculars." "Don't forget…" "Don't forget…" "Don't forget…" But, in spite of all the reminders, everyone knew that someone would forget something. That was the way it always was in the Levy family.

One reminder that was repeated often, perhaps because it was on everyone's mind, was, "David, don't forget your Bar Mitzvah materials." Poppa and Grandma's lake house, where they were heading, would be the perfect place for David to tackle the giant task of learning his Torah portion. He seemed to be having trouble getting started. As for David, he was more intent on making sure that he would remember to take his precious bird recordings. Learning to identify birds and their songs was his passion.

As Judith, David's ten-year-old sister, packed her pink and purple suitcase, she had wonderful visions of the days ahead: fishing on her grandparents' little red and grey pontoon boat named "Knadle" (because it floated just like Grandma's matzo balls); catching giant-sized large and small-mouth bass and little, colorful sunfish; driving the boat while sitting astride Poppa's lap; eating the wonderful foods that Grandma always made especially for them (Judith could just taste those delicious meatballs and giblets); playing the games that were neatly stacked in the basement closet; and those wonderful nature walks with Grandma, gathering wildflowers and learning to identify trees by their leaves and bark. The last item that Judith laid gently in her suitcase was her binoculars, for bird-watching, of course. She especially looked forward to this fun activity with her older brother. David was a whiz at identifying birdcalls and shared all that he knew with his sister. What he couldn't share, however, was his beautiful voice. Judith could learn the calls, but could never repeat them in the same hauntingly beautiful way that David could. His talent was God-given. "I guess God left me out when he was giving out singing voices," she always thought.

Birds were always a big part of vacations with Grandma and Poppa. Judith could remember that as toddlers she and David would run down the beach chasing sea gulls and sandpipers crying out, "Wait for me birds." Of course, catching the birds was never a possibility, but Judith and David were too young and too innocent to realize that.

The vacation house itself was a reflection of their grandparents' love for birds. Carved wooden birds were scattered throughout the house: shore birds on the tables; a swan, a goose, a loon, and a quail family on the walls; and, on the porch, a wounded standing heron whose fragile neck had been broken many times but who had survived multiple surgeries at Poppa's talented hands. On a shelf in the living room, an upright, very proud-looking metal rooster was the newest addition. And what a wonderful ending to a perfect day was the family's gathering on the porch when, at the very moment when light turned to darkness, a whippoorwill would sing his plaintive song, "whip-poor-will, whip-poor-will, whip-poor-will." That was a special treat for Judith and David because it was only recently that they were allowed to stay up that late.

The van packed, the last "don't forgets" said, they were on their way. It was a long trip and they would have to be creative and plan things that would make the time go faster.

"Let's play 'Four-Fourths of a Ghost,' " said David.

"O.K.," Judith answered, even though she knew her brother would usually win. Being older and having a larger vocabulary was not the only reason for David's victories. David had a wonderful way with words—they excited him, and reading, writing, and playing with them gave him great pleasure. "My brother is really special," thought Judith.

After many "Four-Fourths of a Ghost," "Botticelli's," and several rounds of the song "The Parrot in the Tree" that Grandma had composed and Poppa had always enhanced with his great bass voice, they arrived at the lake. There were Poppa and Grandma, with smiles of welcome.

Entering the vacation house for the first time after a long winter was always a happening for Judith and David. The familiarity, the very fact that things did not change, was comforting to them. Today, as always, the shore birds stood proudly on the round table facing the lake, lifelike but whimsical. The metal rooster on the green wall shelf, standing taller than the rest, still seemed to be saying, "Listen to me, guys, I'm the boss."

The swan and quail had their same places on the walls. The loon in the bathroom still had not eaten the wooden berries that were placed at its feet. Only the injured heron, who now sported a red ribbon around his neck to cover his "surgical scars", had changed a bit.

CHAPTER TWO

After everyone had unpacked, Judith and David raced down to the beach with their fishing rods. As usual, Poppa had stored some worms for them in a cottage cheese carton in the refrigerator. It was family lore that once Grandma had opened one of those cartons, expecting to find a tasty dairy lunch, and, instead, was faced with a squirming, wiggling mass of brown earthworms, who were almost as shocked as she was as they were suddenly exposed to the light of day. Now Poppa had to keep them in the old refrigerator in the garage. After baiting their hooks, Judith and David sat down on the dock, dangling their feet in the cool, slightly rippled lake water. They chatted about what they were planning to do in the coming week.

"It's all going to be so much fun," Judith exclaimed excitedly.

"Yeah," said David, "almost all."

"What do you mean?" Judith asked.

"Well, I wish I didn't have to learn my Torah portion. It's turning out to be more difficult than I expected."

Judith had suspected something was interfering with David's Bar Mitzvah progress, but she really didn't understand what. She knew that, in spite of being very smart, David had problems that sometimes interfered with his school work, and that he often needed help at those times. She had heard some people, kids and adults, call him a "special-needs student." "But David was so musical," she thought. "What was there about learning to read from Torah that he could find difficult?" Judith couldn't really know the answer to that. She was only ten and her Bat Mitzvah was still years away.

Suddenly, she felt a strong tug on her fishing line. The red and white bobbin had sunk beneath the water. These were definite signs that a fish was on the line. But it was so heavy!

"David, help," she cried. "I'm not going to be able to bring this one up by myself."

As usual, David was there to help Judith reel in her fish. As the two of them worked to bring it out of the water, the large fish struggled gallantly to release itself from the hook. After much straining and pulling, David and Judith were able to hoist the fish on to the dock and gaze at their prize, a large-mouth bass.

"Hurry, David," said Judith. "Let's get him off the hook. We have to throw him back before he dies."

It was hard work, but when tossed back into the water the fish regained his vigor and quickly swam down to the depths of the lake.

"Thanks David," said Judith. "Thanks for the help."

CHAPTER THREE

It was one of those rainy days at the lake. One of those days that no one really loved because it meant not being able to be outdoors where all their favorite activities took place. Again, as on the drive up to the lake, creativity was called for. Just as Judith and David were about to come up with a plan, Mr. Levy suggested, "David, this is a perfect time to work on your Torah portion. Then, if the rain stops, you kids can resume your outdoor activities."

"OK, Dad," David said dejectedly. He was not a happy boy!

Being left on her own and not liking it, Judith asked, "Can I come up to your room, David?"

"Why not?" David answered. "Company never hurts."

Sitting on his bed, David surrounded himself with the materials he had been given to prepare for "the big occasion": some CD's, a sheet on which there were Hebrew words with strange markings either above or below each of them, and a double-columned page also written in Hebrew.

"What's all this, David?" Judith asked. "It all looks so strange to me. What's that page with all those funny looking signs on it?

These symbols appear below the words in the Chumash:

Mapach   Meircha   Teepcha   Munach   Tvir   Darga

These symbols appear above the words in the Chumash:

Pashta   Katon   Azla   Kadma   Rviee   Zakef Gadol   Gershayim   Tlisha Ktana

Tlish Gdola   Pazeir   Segol   Zarka

Sof Pasuk is at the end of a sentence.

"Those signs or markings are called trope symbols. They are placed either above or below a word of the Chumash or Bible to tell you how to chant that word when you read from the Torah. Each symbol may stand for as little as two or as many as ten musical notes! And, as you can see, each symbol has a name," David said as he pointed to the sheet of tropes.

"How do you know what these notes sound like?" asked Judith.

"That's what the CD's are for," David continued. "Rabbi Stein gave me this sheet with all the tropes and their names on them. On the CD's the Rabbi has sung the tune for each of these tropes. I must learn to match each trope sign with its own tune."

"Wow, that doesn't sound easy," said Judith. "May I listen to the CD's?"

"Sure," said David as he inserted the first CD into the player.

Judith curled up on David's bed as she listened to the strange sounds that filled the room. Each of the tropes had their own names, like "Mapach," "Pashta," "Munach" — words Judith had never heard before, not even in Hebrew School! And David was right; some tropes were made up of many notes. Those were the ones that she thought were really pretty. "Beautiful sounds," thought Judith, "but this is a lot more complicated than I thought."

"Then what is that other page, the one with the Hebrew paragraphs written in two separate columns?" Judith's questions were never-ending.

א תריעו : ובני אהרן הכהנים ^{יּ} הַקָּהָל תִּתְקְעוּ וְלֹא תָרִיעוּ : וּבְנֵי אַהֲרֹן

והיו לכם לחקת עולם לדרתיכם; ^י יִתְקְעוּ בַּחֲצֹצְרוֹת וְהָיוּ לָכֶם לְחֻקַּת עוֹלָם לְדֹ

ה בארצכם על הצר הצרר אתכם ^י וְכִי־תָבֹאוּ מִלְחָמָה בְּאַרְצְכֶם עַל־הַצַּר הַצֹּרֵ

ת ונזכרתם לפני יהוה אלהיכם ^{ייּ} וַהֲרֵעֹתֶם בַּחֲצֹצְרֹת וְנִזְכַּרְתֶּם לִפְנֵי יְהֹוָה

ם: וביום שמחתכם ובמועדיכם ^י וְנוֹשַׁעְתֶּם מֵאֹיְבֵיכֶם : וּבְיוֹם שִׂמְחַתְכֶם וּבְ

ו והקעתם בהצצרת על עלתיכם ^י וּבְרָאשֵׁי חָדְשֵׁכֶּם וּתְקַעְתֶּם בַּחֲצֹצְרֹת עַל

יכם והיו לכם לוכרון לפני ^י וְעַל זִבְחֵי שַׁלְמֵיכֶם וְהָיוּ לָכֶם לְזִכָּרֹ

וה אלהיכם: אֱלֹהֵיכֶם אֲנִי יְהֹוָה אֱלֹהֵיכֶם : פ   חמ

שנית בחדש השני בעשרים ^{חּ} וַיְהִי בַּשָּׁנָה הַשֵּׁנִית בַּחֹדֶשׁ הַשֵּׁנִי בְּ

הענן מעל משכן העדת: ויסעו ^{יּ} בָּחֹדֶשׁ נַעֲלָה הֶעָנָן מֵעַל מִשְׁכַּן הָעֵדֻת

למסעיהם ממדבר סיני וישכן ^{חּ} בְּנֵי־יִשְׂרָאֵל לְמַסְעֵיהֶם מִמִּדְבַּר סִינָי

פארן : ויסעו בראשנה על פי ^פ הֶעָנָן בְּמִדְבַּר פָּארָן : וַיִּסְעוּ בָּרִאשֹׁנָה

ה: ויסע דגל מחנה בני יהודה ^{חּ} יְהֹוָה בְּיַד־מֹשֶׁה : וַיִּסַּע דֶּגֶל מַחֲנֵה בְּנֵי

"Well," David said, trying to keep his explanations as clear and understandable as possible, "that page is called a 'Tikkun.' It's supposed to be a helper to me. On it is my Torah portion. You've noticed that the page is divided into two sections."

"Yes. Why is that?" asked Judith.

"Well, you can see that on the left side of the page the Hebrew words have vowels under them. They also have additional little markings either above or below them. That's what the pages of the Chumash or Bible look like when we study it in Hebrew school. Do those additional markings look familiar to you?"

"Yes!" exclaimed Judith, excited that she was beginning to understand. "Those are the same signs that are on the first sheet we looked at, the one with the trope symbols. They are there to tell you how to chant those words when you are singing your Torah portion."

"You're catching on," said David, pleased that he was explaining it well.

"But what is on the other side of the page, the right column?" Judith asked.

"Look at the two sides, Judith, and tell me how they are different," challenged David. Judith ran her eyes across both sides of the page, first one line, then another. Then it came to her. "The right side has no vowels and no trope signs. Why are they missing?" Judith wondered out loud.

"They are missing because that is exactly the way the Torah is written," David answered. "On your Bar or Bat Mitzvah day you cannot use the

Tikkun. You must read directly from the Torah, which, you have just learned, has neither notes nor vowels, just like the right column of the Tikkun," David continued.

"How can you do that without the vowels and trope signs? That sounds so difficult!" Judith suddenly understood the huge task that David was facing.

"You must just remember what the tune is supposed to be, what you've learned from the Tikkun," David answered with a sigh, satisfied that he had completed the explanation well.

"Oh, my!" exclaimed Judith. "That sounds awfully hard. Have you gotten that far? Is that the part you find so difficult? It would be for me!"

"No," said David sadly. "I haven't even gotten to that point. I can't learn the notes. I can't make a connection between the trope symbols and their tunes."

There was a brief silence as Judith mulled over the significance of David's admission. Then, she said with determination, "You'll do it, David. I know you can. We'll figure out a way."

The sun began to come out.

CHAPTER FOUR

As Judith was getting ready for bed that night, she thought with excitement about the bird watching she and David planned to do the next day. They hadn't done it for a while and it would be fun to see if there were any new birds around the lake house. She also thought about David's confession to her. That he could not learn the Torah trope was very worrisome to her. "Maybe tomorrow we'll come up with a solution," she thought. David and Judith were used to helping each other out of tough spots, but this one seemed especially hard.

As Judith got under the covers, she heard David call out from the next room, "Sweet dreams, Judith."

"Sweet dreams to you too," Judith called back. It was difficult for Judith to know whether her dream that night was sweet because she really didn't understand it. In the dream, she saw, fluttering above her, those strange little trope markings that she had seen earlier. They were carried in the beaks of brightly colored, strange-looking birds. She could hear each of the birds singing its own trope melody. What resulted was a symphony of sounds, as beautiful as it was strange.

When she awoke the next morning, Judith remembered her dream. "What did it all mean?" she wondered. Soon she gave up trying to figure it out and said to herself what Great-Grandma Bea used to say when either she didn't have an answer or she didn't want to think about a problem: "Whatever." Whatever the meaning of the dream, now was the time for bird-watching.

CHAPTER FIVE

It was a beautiful sunny morning and the hour was perfect for discovering birds. Long awake and already engaged in their morning activities, the birds were chattering and singing away. With their binoculars in hand, Judith and David eagerly set out to meet old acquaintances and perhaps make some new ones. And, if they did encounter birds they had neither seen nor heard before, David had his cell phone with which to enter their calls.

"David is so relaxed this morning. Birds do that to him," Judith observed. "His Bar Mitzvah worries seem to have left him, at least for a while." She was happy to see his smiling face.

It was not difficult for them to recognize the first bird call. "It's a wild turkey," they both exclaimed. Sure enough, as they turned their heads, there he was. Having come down from a tree where he roosted all night, he was spending his daylight hours on the ground, searching for some vegetable morsels, perhaps even some insects, or possibly that special prize, a juicy salamander.

For Judith, the turkey gobble had always been rather ordinary, not really anything special. Today she heard it differently. It was not just a gobble. It had a pattern: first a series of four notes, followed by a stream of descending notes that went down the scale at high speed.

"That's cool," she thought. "Birds are kind of like musicians, with their own notes and their own rhythms."

"Well, that must be about the 200th time we've seen or heard one of those," David said, unimpressed by this find.

"But I've never heard it this way before," Judith said to herself. This time was different.

They continued to walk, as the symphony of birdcalls followed them. Suddenly, ahead of them appeared what would be their find of the day. Perched high in a tree, waiting for its prey, was a red-shouldered hawk. Was he pondering his menu for the day—a mouse, a chipmunk, a frog, or perhaps a fellow bird? Judith and David stood still, hoping that this beautiful, long-winged bird would not fly away. They wanted to observe him, but they also wanted to hear his call. Unfortunately, after gazing at them for a minute, the hawk made his preparations for takeoff. Then, flashing his red shoulders and bright white-spotted wings, he soared above them. But they were lucky. As he made his getaway he uttered the hoarse screech that they had heard only twice before. And, like the turkey gobble, this time Judith heard it differently. It was not just a song but sounds that descended in a clear, note-by-note slide. David imitated it in his beautiful voice and they laughed as they followed the bird's flight.

As they walked on, Judith and David were accompanied by the familiar "coo" of the Mourning Dove.

"Boy, it sure sounds like he's in mourning," David said. "I guess that's how he got his name."

For Judith, the plaintive call had new meaning. Now she realized that it had two parts, each with three notes. It was more complex than the hawk's, more like the turkey's.

"Some birds are better song writers than others," she thought. She gazed up at this sleek, greyish-brown bird with his long pointed tail and black dotted wings. She noticed that, as he uttered his perching "coo" on the tree branch above them, he was puffing out his throat and bobbing his tail in rhythm. "Quite a performer," she thought.

Tired and hot from their long walk, Judith and David sat down under a large oak tree near a stream, a place where they had often rested. David, never wanting to waste a minute, searched the area with his binoculars. Focusing high in the treetops he made his discovery. "Judith," he said quietly, "there is a nest in that tree. It's made of bark and weeds and it has at least three greenish eggs with brown markings on them. I can't be sure just how many. Look in your binoculars. Do you see the nest?"

"Yes," Judith answered as she scanned the tree with her binoculars. "Now let's look to see if there is a bird nearby, because eggs are not left unattended for long." As they scanned the same branch, they saw it! It was a Cerulean Warbler, with his black-and-blue-streaked top feathers and white bars on his wings.

"Shh," David cautioned. "Remember his call? Let's see if he will sing for us." Judith did remember and hoped she could hear it again. After a few minutes, there it was: three or four of the same notes and then a rapid slide upward of many notes. High in the canopy of the tree, repeating his song many times, the warbler had granted his young listeners a concert. This song sounded familiar to Judith. She had heard it before but she was almost sure it hadn't come from a bird.

After many birds, many songs, and a few more rests, the birdwatchers were ready to call it a day. "I'm hungry," David finally admitted. "Let's have lunch."

"Fine with me," agreed Judith.

As Judith got ready for bed that night, her favorite bird song found its way through the open window and flooded her room. "Whip-poor-will, whip-poor-will, whip-poor-will." These glorious sounds were no surprise to her because most evenings at the lake house, when the very last moments of light fade into darkness, this very mysterious male bird chants his repetitive three-note strain. Judith and David, like most people, even more experienced bird watchers, had never seen a whippoorwill. Because it is so well camouflaged by tree leaves and branches, and because it stays still and silent during the day, it is known mostly by its familiar mating call.

Sinking into her soft pillow while pulling up the covers, Judith began to mull over the activities of the last two days. She wondered about where she had heard the tune of the Cerulean Warbler before and pondered the meaning of last night's dream. The birds carrying trope signs in their beaks, fluttering above her as they uttered their melodies, and David's repeating the many bird songs as they walked through the fields and woodlands that morning —it all seemed to mesh in her mind. And then, there it was! The answer to David's problem. "I've got it," she thought. "I have the solution."

Darkness set in as the whippoorwill ended his song. Judith fell fast asleep. There was an unmistakable smile on her face.

CHAPTER SIX

The next morning when David asked his usual, "What should we do today?" Judith did not answer with *her* usual, "I don't know; what do you want to do?" Today she had a plan, and the sooner they started on it the better. Not wanting to reveal everything at once, she said, "Let's go up to your room, David, I have a fun project for us to work on."

As they walked to his room, David wondered why Judith was being so mysterious about this new project. "What's so special about my room?" he asked.

"You'll see," Judith promised.

When they got there, Judith told David to take out the CD's on which the Rabbi had recorded the tropes, or melodies, for his Torah reading. "This is supposed to be fun?" David thought. "Studying for my Bar Mitzvah is not my idea of fun," he said to himself.

"Now, David, get out your phone with all the bird calls that we have heard." David followed her instructions, still wondering where this was going.
"OK, first we are going to play the CD's with the trope melodies. As we listen to them, let's try to think if there are any bird calls that sound similar to

any one of these tropes?"

"Oh, it's a game she has made up," David thought. Some of Judith's games were a bit childish, but this one sounded like it might be fun.

David started the CD. It was not long before he shouted, "The trope called 'Revii' sounds a lot like the song of the Red Shouldered Hawk we saw today. You know, the way his call slides down the scale."

"You're right, David. Let's check it out on the phone." When they found the song of this magnificent predatory bird, they giggled at the similarity between this song of nature and the man-made tune. David was psyched. Judith's plan was working.

And so, the two "investigators" continued on, first listening to the Hebrew tropes, then drawing bird calls from their memories, and finally checking with their recorded bird calls. When they listened carefully, they were amazed to discover that there were so many tropes that resembled bird songs! The beginning of the Mourning Dove's song was like the "Pashta" trope, while the beginning of the Robin's song was definitely a "Mapach." And the song of the talented Black Skimmer combined both the "Mapach" and the "Pashta" tropes.

"Wow, this is fun," David applauded Judith's new game. "How did you think of it?"

"It was in a dream," Judith said, not wanting to go any further yet. "Let's keep it a game for a while longer," she thought.

"Gosh," David said, "Did you hear that Cerulean Warbler call? How do you like that for a 'Tlisha Gdola?' The notes go upward in the same way! The songs of the Grey Jay and Pileated Woodpecker do that too."

The morning went by as Judith and David, excited by the joy of discovery, found more and more tropes that had birdsong equivalents. The Bald Eagle was a decided "Darga Tvir" and the Wild Turkey that they had visited yesterday morning, along with the Yellow Warbler and Field Sparrow, were definite "Zakef Gadols." And that glorious Whippoorwill chant that accompanied Judith to bed was an "Etnachta" in bird song. The Wood Thrush sounded like the "Kadma" and "Azla" combination. Perhaps the best match of all was the Grey Jay's song with the complicated trope "Pazeir."

"I wonder if some Rabbi, hundreds of years ago, was sitting outside his home with birds singing around him as he wrote the Torah tropes," David said. "Were birds the inspiration for all this?"

Judith thought of her dream of the winged tropes flying above her. David's idea was a definite possibility. She also thought that now was the time for the next step.

CHAPTER SEVEN

David could have gone on all day with the matching game. Although Judith was having a lot of fun too, she wanted to know if all this could be helpful to David in his Bar Mitzvah preparation. She suspected it could but didn't know how. But, before she could even ask that question, David had the answer.

"You know, Judith, if they had bird pictures next to the words of the Torah instead of trope signs, Torah reading would be a cinch for me," he said with a twinkle in his eye, thinking he was only joking.

But Judith didn't smile. She thought of her dream. That was the answer! But could it be done? And how?

David, seeing that his sister did not laugh at his "joke" but instead stayed serious and silent, realized that he had latched on to something. He paused, thought a little, and then exclaimed, "Judith, that's it. I can do it."

"Do what?" she asked, not sure of what he meant.

"If I could substitute bird pictures for the trope signs, I could learn my Torah portion! I know the bird songs by heart, so whenever I see each picture

I will know how to chant the word. Do you think it would work, Judith?" he asked eagerly.

"I know it would," Judith answered, again seeing in her mind the trope-carrying birds of her dream.

"Will you help?" he asked.

"I will do anything you tell me to do," she answered very willingly.

In the days that followed, David and Judith worked diligently with their grandparents' computer and many bird books. They were able to do what they had planned. They created a page of Torah, speckled with bird pictures that would guide David in the chanting of his portion. Instead of the trope sign near the words, a picture of the bird with the matching song was put in its place. Then, making use of the newly created page, David was able to quickly learn one paragraph of his Torah portion.

"David, it sounds like you have really been making progress with your Torah portion," his dad said one afternoon while playing a family game of Scrabble. "We've been listening to the chanting coming from your room. I guess bringing your Bar Mitzvah materials to the lake house was a good idea."

"It was a great idea," answered David as he winked to his smiling sister.

Judith and David spent the rest of their lake vacation doing the things that they loved: fishing, boating, and bird watching. Every day David practiced chanting his Torah portion, which pleased his parents, grandparents, and especially Judith. She never had her flying trope dream again, but she never doubted its meaning.

On the way home from the lake at their vacation's end, David thought about his first meeting with the Rabbi that was coming up next week. He was excited to be able to show the Rabbi how much of his Torah portion he had learned. He was fearful, too, that it would not be good enough.

CHAPTER EIGHT

As he biked his way to the synagogue, David thought about how Rabbi Stein might react to his Torah reading. "Will he disapprove of the way I have learned it? Will he tell me start all over again and just memorize it as I would a song?" David wasn't sure.

"Come in, David," Rabbi Stein said as he welcomed David into his study. "Have a seat."

David looked around and saw the many books that crowded the Rabbi's shelves. Some new and bright, some old and weathered, many with gilded Hebrew letters, others with simple English titles—the Rabbi's collection was impressive. David liked Rabbi Stein very much and respected him for his knowledge and his kindness.

"So, how was your vacation at your grandparents' summer home?" the Rabbi asked.

"Great," David replied. "I had a lot of fun."

"Wonderful, wonderful," Rabbi Stein commented as he sorted some papers on his desk. "Vacations are good for us. They provide rest for our minds.

Often, when I return from my vacation, I can think more clearly and can solve problems that I wasn't able to before. Do you agree, David?"

"You're right," David answered, thinking of that afternoon in his room at the lake with Judith, comparing the trope melodies to bird calls.

"Well, I'm glad you had a good time," Rabbi Stein continued, "and were you able to make some progress in learning your Torah portion?"

David hesitated. "Well, I did have some problems in learning the trope…"

Rabbi Stein interrupted, "You know, David, you don't have to learn the trope. You could just learn your portion as one learns a song. You could memorize it from a CD that I would give you."

"I don't want to do that, Rabbi. I want to learn the melodies from a symbol, just as my father, grandfather and all those who came before me did. I want to be part of that tradition. It's important to me."

From there David went on to explain how he was able to connect his love of and knowledge about birds to learning his portion, how he and Judith compared trope tunes to bird songs. He then showed the Rabbi the revised pages of his Torah reading, with bird pictures replacing the trope signs. David couldn't tell if the quizzical look on the Rabbi's face was one of curiosity or disapproval.

"I'd like to hear what you have learned," Rabbi Stein said. "Chant for me."

In his clear, smooth voice, David began his Torah reading.

The birds on the pages acted as both his guides and his cheerleaders as he glided smoothly from one line to another. He delivered, without any mistakes, what he had rehearsed many times with his sister as his audience.

As he finished his chanting David looked up at the Rabbi. "Was that a tear in his eye?" David asked himself. "What is he going to say?"

"David, that was beautiful," Rabbi Stein said. "It was both traditional and unique. You have done an amazing job. You have not changed the tradition; you have enhanced it." He continued, "Did you know that many people think that a very long time ago, when a person read from the Torah, a learned man would give him hand signals that would tell him how to chant each word? Later, trope signs replaced those hand signals. And, David, you have replaced the trope signs with bird pictures! The trope chant is over 2000 years old. This is the tradition that you have become a part of."

"But more important than that," Rabbi Stein went on, "is the fact that Jews took this, what is called their 'cantillation system,' wherever they went. Because of that, tropes in different geographic locations differed from each other. They were influenced by the musical styles of their particular area. And so, there is the Ashkenazic, the Sephardic, the Moroccan, the Syrian, the Baghdadian and Yemenite tropes. What is more, ALL are acceptable in any synagogue in the world."

"Wow," David said. "That's just like bird calls. Did you know that the call of a certain bird can be different depending on where he lives? Birds can have different dialects depending on where they come from."

"No, I didn't know that." The Rabbi looked astonished. "I guess this is just another example of how humans often mirror the natural world around them."

"Kind of like how the trope sounds mirror the bird calls," David said as he continued the Rabbi's thought.

"Just like that," agreed the Rabbi. "So you have continued a tradition in a very beautiful and special way." Rabbi Stein went on. "In chapter 119, verse 54 of Psalms, one of our holy books, it says, "Your laws have been songs for me in my dwelling place'. You have sung God's words with your songs, David, in *your* dwelling place. You have chanted His words in a way that reflects who you are, what your talents are, and what you can do in the service of God. That is what "my dwelling place' means. We all do God's work in our own ways, according to our own abilities. You should be very proud of yourself, David. I certainly am."

And David *was* very proud of himself. It made him happy to know that he had both the Rabbi's approval and his blessing. When they learned how David had accomplished this, his parents were especially proud too. In the days and weeks ahead, he worked hard to complete his Torah portion, first learning it with his beloved birds pointing the way, and then gradually learning to do without them as he became more and more familiar with the reading. When his Bar Mitzvah day arrived, he was ready to chant his portion as no one had ever done before him. And he was proud of that too!

CHAPTER NINE

Standing on the bimah that Saturday morning, as he gazed at the scroll that the Rabbi unfurled before him, David was not alone. Although they could not actually enter the synagogue with him, there were his birds, fluttering their wings across the page of the scroll, finding their ways to their proper words. Then, with a blink of his eye, they were gone, and David was on his own. He easily chanted the portion that had so intimidated him months before. His sweet voice flooded the synagogue with sounds of nature that had become intertwined with words of Torah.

In his Dvar Torah, David, as all Bar Mitzvah boys do, thanked his teachers, the Rabbi, his parents and grandparents. And then finally, and with great emotion, he gave a special thanks to his sister, Judith, for her support, her love, her joy, and for sharing everything with him, even her dreams.

It was a wonderful day for the entire Levy family. As Judith walked over to give her brother a congratulatory kiss, an elderly lady gently squeezed her arm and said, "You should be very proud of your brother, Judith. He sings just like a bird."

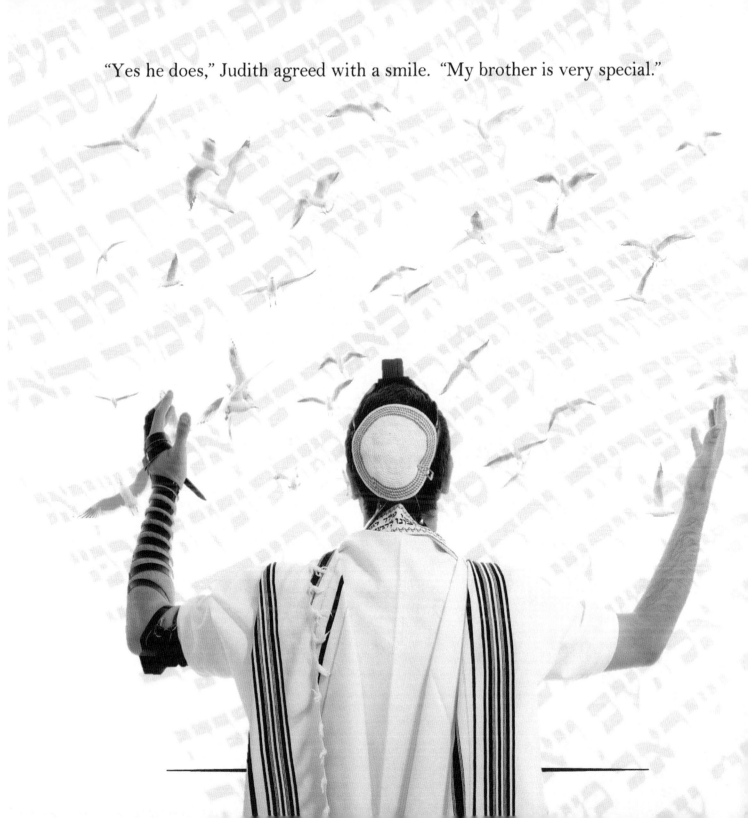

"Yes he does," Judith agreed with a smile. "My brother is very special."

CALEB, THE OKETZ DOG

The man and the dog stared at each other. The man appeared frustrated and helpless. The dog looked confused and sad, his head cocked to one side, his body otherwise still.

"Okay, Caleb," the uniformed man announced with a sigh. "Looks like today is no different than any other day. You just won't obey any of my commands."

However, because he enjoyed the dog's company, the man invited his canine friend to a unique celebration that would soon take place in town. "Let's go downtown. It's the first night of Hanukah and there will be a candle-lighting ceremony in the Capitol rotunda."

Although there were few Jews in Helena, Montana, Captain Dart, a policeman who was not Jewish, knew that there would be a crowd, as people from all over the state would attend this event.

Captain Dart fastened Caleb's leash and the two made their way to the police car that would take them to the Capitol. A few minutes later, his hands on the steering wheel, his eyes straight ahead, Dart's thoughts soon turned to something that happened years ago in Helena.

It was 1993, on one of the eight nights of Hanukah. In the windows of Jewish homes throughout the town, one could see menorahs bearing flickering candles that announced the miracle of the holiday. However, later that night, in a terrible action by vandals, these very same windows were broken, shattering the calm and serenity of the holiday. The modern miracle of the holiday occurred soon afterward when thousands of non-Jewish townspeople put menorahs in their own windows, making it impossible for anyone to tell which were Jewish homes and which were not. In this way the Jewish families were protected from future harm. Officer Dart smiled as he remembered that because of this action by the community, the vandalism stopped. "Sometimes the people themselves do a better job of protecting each other than we do," he mused. Hanukah had a very special significance in Montana after that.

When they arrived at the Capitol, Captain Dart and Caleb headed for the building's rotunda, where the candle lighting would take place. The crowd had already gathered and there was silence as the Shamash candle was lit and then it, in turn, was used to light the lone first-night candle. Caleb seemed even more interested than the officer. "Strange dog," thought Captain Dart. "Sometimes he seems more human than dog."

As Dart looked over the crowd, he noticed a bearded man wearing a black hat and a long black coat. The officer must have also caught the man's attention because the oddly dressed gentleman soon began to stroll over to the policeman and his dog.

"That's a nice dog you have there," he said to the Captain. "A Belgian Malinois, I believe."

Surprised that the man was able to recognize this uncommon breed, Captain Dart answered, "Yes, I think so, but he's not as smart as he is supposed to be. He doesn't respond to any of my commands."

Caleb trotted over to the Rabbi and started to lick the man's hands. The Rabbi uttered a few non-intelligible words to him, and Caleb rubbed himself affectionately against the man's legs.

"I am Rabbi Tracht," said the bearded man. "I suspect that your dog has a very interesting story," he announced mysteriously.

CHAPTER TWO

Caleb's story began in an animal shelter in Holland. He wasn't a puppy picked up off the streets because his owner didn't want him anymore. Nor was he a stray dog whose homeless mother gave birth to him in a cold, deserted alley. Caleb was born in this particular shelter, where many of the dogs would each bring to their owner a price of $3500 to $10,000! They were Belgian Malinois, also sometimes known as Belgian Shepherds, dogs that were originally bred to herd and guard sheep in Belgium. But shepherding was not going to be Caleb's fate. Because dogs of his breed were known to be super-intelligent, loyal, agile, sensitive, versatile, and protective of their masters, Caleb would be selected for much more dangerous work.

"This looks like a good one," a man who wore a red beret and red boots said as he pointed to Caleb. "Have there been any problems with him?"

"No," said the kennel manager. "He seems very bright and has been quite healthy."

"Good, then we'll take him," said the red-hatted man.

Caleb's ears pricked up as he listened intently to the conversation, but flattened as soon as he sensed that something new was about to happen to him.

The man with the red hat put a collar and leash on him and the two of them, man and dog, walked away from the shelter together. A new life was waiting for Caleb.

Caleb mostly slept during the plane ride to who-knows-where. During the moments when his eyes were open, he seemed comforted to see that nearby were Toshi, Cali, Motze, Ray, Elvis and Taffy, his friends from the kennel. At least some things were familiar in this strange adventure!

After landing in Israel, it was a long truck ride to where they were going. Caleb and his friends, all active and athletic dogs, were not used to being still for so long. The red-hatted man seemed to know this and took turns petting and cuddling each of them while feeding them ice chips. Finally they arrived at a place called Adam. They were in central Israel.

At first, their destination looked like an ordinary army base. Upon closer examination, however, there were strange indications that it was more than just that. On the buildings were signs that said "No urinating on walls!" Dustpans were lying around everywhere. What were they meant to pick up? Gazing into one of the buildings one could see dogs walking on treadmills! As they walked on, with a beautiful view of the Judean hills in front of them, they reached an enclosed grassy area that appeared to be a cemetery. It was very strange though that among the gravestones was a large sculpture of a dog and a man. On it was the inscription, "Walk softly, for here lie soldiers of Israel." But the names inscribed on the tombstones did not sound like soldiers' names! They were names like "Jerzy," "Senna," "Frenchy." The "soldiers," it seemed, were dogs. What kind of place was this? And why was Caleb here?

CHAPTER THREE

At the top of the hill in front of them stood more buildings. Waiting for them near one of the buildings was a woman dressed just like the man who accompanied Caleb to Israel and who was with him now. Also wearing a red beret and red boots, she walked toward Caleb with a welcoming smile and then stopped before she reached him.

"Shalom and welcome to Oketz, the K-9 unit of the Israel Defense Forces," she said to the dog, waiting for him to give her the inspection that she knew would be coming. Knowing that he would be fearful of strangers, she was careful not to overwhelm him with her affection.

"My name is Liat and we are going to be very good friends." Then, turning to the man, she asked, "Does he have a name or should I give him one?"

"He is called Caleb," said the man. "But, if you wish, you may rename him."

"Hmm, Caleb, you say. I like that name. It sounds like 'Kelev', the Hebrew name for dog. How appropriate. Besides, Caleb was a very important man in the Bible. He was one of the twelve spies who God sent into Canaan to report on what was there. Ten spies warned that the Hebrews should not go into the land because giants lived there whom they surely could not defeat.

Joshua and Caleb were the only ones who did not lose faith. They expressed their confidence that God would deliver Canaan into their hands. For this God rewarded them. They were the only adult males who left Egypt that were allowed to enter the land. God called Caleb 'my servant,' and while you will not be my servant, Caleb, you will be my friend. And we will be inseparable. Yes, definitely, Liat and Caleb will be a team."

As they walked past the dog "dormitory" that would be Caleb's home for many years, Liat thought about what had brought her to this day. As a member of a unit of soldiers who patrolled the border between Israel and Jordan, she was asked if she wanted to try out for Oketz, a special unit of the Israel Defense Forces that specializes in training and handling dogs for military uses. Because Liat never had a dog but always yearned for one, she happily accepted the offer. Now, as she strolled with her new friend, her thoughts turned to how she and Caleb would learn to care for and trust each other.

Liat looked down at Caleb as they headed for their first destination. His eyes, brown, medium-sized and almond-shaped, seemed intelligent and curious, traits that were typical of his breed. His black nose, black, triangular erect ears and black mask were a stunning contrast to his rich fawn-colored, short and straight coat that was itself highlighted with black tips. A peek at his underside revealed a lighter but equally beautiful fawn color. Liat knew that his coat was one of the traits that made Caleb's breed ideal for the task that was ahead of him. It was weather resistant and not too heavy for the warm climate of Israel. His size would also be an advantage since Malinois dogs are small enough to be carried if injured, a possibility Liat knew could very well happen.

"What a handsome guy my new partner is," she thought proudly. "How cute it is that although we have not yet given him a collar, the longer hair around his neck looks like a collar. A sign, perhaps, that his destiny is to serve man (or woman)?" she asked herself.

Their first stop was the clinic, where a veterinarian would examine Caleb and prescribe an exercise program for him. Dr. Ben-Zeev was there waiting for them.

"Good morning, Liat," he said. "Is this your new partner?"

"Yes, doctor," Liat replied. "He just arrived and it seems like he is raring to go."

"I'm sure he is," Dr. Ben-Zeev agreed. "As you know, Belgian Malinois dogs need a great deal of exercise and mental stimulation. He has been quite inactive on the long plane ride to Israel. We'd better get him started right away. He needs to vent his energy and keep his mind occupied while performing interesting tasks, so let's get this examination over with quickly."

"Hmm," thought Liat, who was also super active and got bored easily, "This dog sounds more and more like me."

Dr. Ben-Zeev found Caleb to be in excellent health and ready for training. "As he trains," the doctor revealed, "we will care for him just as if he were a professional athlete. We will control his diet, exercise him in the gym, and have him walk with you at least twice a day. He will become an Oketz dog; we will care for him as he prepares for his job of caring for and protecting us."

Liat had been preparing for this day for 18 months. With dogs that were already seasoned soldiers, she learned about the commands, the rewards, the loving care, the dangers—all the knowledge that she would need to train Caleb for his job as a canine soldier of Israel. Liat was ready. Now her job was to make Caleb ready.

CHAPTER FOUR

Liat arose bright and early every morning, eager to begin the day's exciting and challenging job of training Caleb for what would eventually be his very important job in the Israel Defense Forces, otherwise known as the IDF or the Israeli Army. Caleb was to be trained as a bomb sniffer. For many years Oketz dogs had been able to prevent hundreds of suicide attacks in central Israel. Hopefully, Caleb would join their ranks, saving both soldiers and Israeli citizens. However, it would be a long while before Caleb and Liat would be ready for that.

Not all of Caleb's friends were being trained to be bomb sniffers. Motze was learning how to be an attack dog; Cali's job would be to rescue soldiers who were kidnapped, captured or imprisoned; Taffy's duty would be to search for guns and munitions. Ray and Elvis would be drug- detection dogs, and Toshi would help track down and chase enemy attackers.

As a bright, alert, and energetic one-year-old puppy, Caleb was just the right age to start his training. Before he could learn to be a bomb sniffer, however, there were basic things that he and Liat had to accomplish. Most important in the early days was that Liat and Caleb had to learn to trust each other. They had to develop a strong bond because of the life-and-death situations in which they could find themselves. They would become "battle buddies." Caleb had to realize that Liat was his friend, as well as his teacher and handler. Learning to obey her, even in stressful or exciting situations, was a key part of his training. For Liat it was most important that, through her handling of him, she could be sure of his loyalty and his desire to protect her.

What Caleb found most difficult was learning to ignore the noise of bombs and gunfire on the base. He was a long way from the Dutch shelter where he was born, where the only noises were the barking of his many friends and the opening and closing of their cages.

As the days and weeks went by, Caleb continued his strenuous workouts in the gym, running on the treadmill just as if he were an athlete in training. Liat worked with him to build his endurance, but she was always careful not to jeopardize his health in the process. She worried that he would fracture his legs, as some of the Oketz dogs had done. What was most surprising to Liat was that through all of this rigorous training Caleb had never bitten her. She had been warned that this might happen, but she was lucky. "We were made for each other," she thought with a smile.

Caleb and Liat became close friends, so close that it was difficult for her to leave him each evening. When she went home for the Jewish High Holidays, the veterinarian noticed signs of sadness and anxiety in Caleb because of the separation. When she returned to the base, she tried to make it up to him by giving him frequent belly rubs, which always comforted him.

Caleb learned by regular, consistent repetition. Since rewards were very important in his training, he was given a toy or a chance to play a fetching game when he performed well. Tug-of-war was also a favorite of his. Most of all, he learned by seeking and gaining Liat's approval. "Very good" and "excellent" were words that he sought and received many times. He could even read Liat's facial expressions and her body language and could, in this way, detect signs of disapproval. He was so good at doing this that Liat often felt that he was reading her mind! "He is one step ahead of me," she thought, "and that could be dangerous. I have to be smarter than he is. I have to stay one step ahead of him." And that was not always easy.

Caleb was a happy dog during these early days of general training. With regular opportunities to vent his energy and to use his mind to do interesting things, he never became bored. Boredom is a "no-no" for Malinois dogs, for when they become bored and frustrated they frequently bark a lot and destroy things by chewing on them. Knowing also the need for Caleb to become socialized, Liat made sure that he would be exposed to many friendly people. Soon he was able to distinguish them from the "bad guys" he would someday encounter.

The important day finally arrived. The most basic of his training was over and now the bomb-sniffing exercises would begin. Now a generally well-trained dog, Caleb would start on his program to become a specialist.

CHAPTER FIVE

Liat was amazed at what she had learned in her training, that the ability of a dog to sniff a scent is 1,000 times greater than that of a human! She would use Caleb's "super nose," together with his natural drive for retrieval, to make him a successful bomb sniffer. The days seemed to fly by as Caleb learned to detect the active explosive materials in various kinds of bombs through their scent. In the days that followed, Liat trained him to find a certain scent by rewarding him when he did. As before, often the reward would merely be another retrieval game with a toy. When Liat would take away the toy, Caleb would go back to searching for the scent because he looked forward to being rewarded again with another toy retrieval game. Food was not what Caleb wanted; he wanted fun, games, and Liat's approval. Every day Liat showed Caleb how much she loved him. And every day she loved him more. The hardest part for her was knowing that his job could entail his giving up his life for her and others.

The hardest part for Caleb was wearing the paraphernalia that was necessary in order to receive Liat's commands from a distance. It was necessary for him to wear a collar that had a radio in it, and a camera and walkie-talkie on his leg to relay information back to her or to other soldiers. In her hand, Liat would hold a communications device with which she gave orders to Caleb, who could hear them on the device that was connected to his collar.

Every day, real explosives were hidden from view—in cabinets, under airplane seats, in luggage, in a field. Soon Caleb learned to pick up their scent in seconds. Liat had to teach him to sit immediately when he found the scent so that he would not harm himself by attempting to retrieve the bombs. "Good Caleb," she would say, "but don't bring it to me!"

It was important that Caleb learn how to respond to a bomb explosion. For this purpose, he was exposed to many controlled detonations while in training. Liat would shout, "Fire in the hole" to warn Caleb of a detonation, and he learned to understand that warning very well.

Meanwhile, Motze, Caleb's best friend at the shelter in Holland, was being trained to be an attack dog. His trainer, Gilad, would put on a thick padded coat and pretend to be a runaway suspect. Motze would run after him and sink his teeth into his well-padded arm, slamming him to the ground. He held Gilad until he was ordered to release him. They did this many times until Motze was ready for the real action of searching for and attacking suspects.

Soon Caleb was ready for "work." In the beginning, he and Liat were stationed at checkpoints between the West Bank and Israel, and Caleb's job was to detect any explosives in cars going through them. On his first day on the job, while sniffing an SUV, he suddenly sat up and looked at Liat. After a quick search, a bomb was discovered. "Good, good," Liat congratulated Caleb as she threw him a ball. As usual, a happy game of fetch followed.

At other times, Caleb was called in to check events like concerts, soccer games and political rallies which important dignitaries would attend. In less than one year, he detected 50 bombs, saving many innocent people's lives.

Although there were many close calls, Caleb was one of the lucky dogs. He survived with his life. The day that Liat would never forget was one of those close calls. The Givati Brigade soldiers and the Engineering Corps troops were out on a routine operation when they came under gunfire. They knew from which house the shots were fired but did not want to enter it until the arrival of the Oketz team. Liat and Caleb arrived soon after the call for help. Because a dog must walk ahead of the soldiers, sacrificing himself if necessary for their protection, Liat unleashed Caleb, who then began to search the house. When he began to bark, Liat knew that a terrorist, possibly a bomber, was hiding inside. But where? On what floor? In what room? Under these conditions it would be very dangerous to send in a soldier; he would be an easy target for a hidden terrorist. Liat, using her handheld communications device, gave her orders to Caleb, who could hear them on the device that was attached to his collar. Caleb got the message and barked in the direction of one room. Unfortunately though, his bark alerted the terrorists to his presence, and a shot from the room was directed at him. The soldiers, confident in what Caleb had "told" them and aware of the direction from which the shot had come, discovered the terrorists cowering in an underground chamber which was stashed with weapons and bombs. Fortunately, because of his quick movements, Caleb, although wounded seriously enough to require surgery and medical treatment at the Oketz hospital, recovered quickly. Liat gave Caleb lots of love while he was recovering, and soon he was back on the job, being rewarded time after time with his favorite game of fetch.

"Without Caleb we would never have found the underground room and would not have been able to capture the men and locate the bombs," said Captain Dov Goshen, Liat's commanding officer. "He saved many lives, while risking his own."

Not all of Caleb's friends were so lucky. Early one morning the IDF intelligence learned that an important Hamas terrorist, Abdul Nasser, who was responsible for two bombing attacks that killed 19 people, was hiding out in a small village near Nablus. This was at a time when the army was desperately trying to find terrorists in order to prevent suicide attacks. The country was still very much in shock from the suicide bombing of a bus which had occurred just two weeks before, killing 15 people.

The Paratroopers Brigade, with some troops from the Naval Commandos, was assigned the job of locating and capturing Nasser. It was not going to be easy. Nasser had escaped arrest three times before. The army commanders asked for additional soldiers and dogs from Oketz. One of those dogs was Toshi.

The team arrived at al-Pundak, the small village where Nasser was believed to be in hiding. For hours they searched homes and other buildings but were unsuccessful. The soldiers were tired and frustrated. Suddenly, Toshi seemed to be detecting something unusual in a nearby bush. Yossi, Toshi's handler, unleashed him so that he could get closer to the bush. As he neared the suspicious area, Toshi began scratching the ground, his way of communicating to Yossi his feelings of danger. Seconds later, Nasser appeared and fired two shots at the brave dog, killing him immediately. Toshi was a hero that day; when Nasser shot him, the IDF soldiers were able to return the fire successfully and the terrorist was killed.

Like soldiers who had fallen, Toshi was not left behind on the battlefield. Yossi lovingly carried him "home," tears filling his eyes when he thought of the days ahead without his best friend. He was consoled by his Oketz commander, Lt. Col. Barak, who comforted him with, "When a dog gets killed that is not a success, but it does mean that he did his job. Toshi did his job. He protected us. You trained him well for that."

Toshi received a military funeral, not unlike the funerals that were given for a soldier. Yossi, his friends and his family all came to pay their last respects to their noble friend. Lt. Col. Barak presented Yossi with a medal for Toshi's exceptional performance, and Yossi's father, who was a rabbi, offered some appropriate prayers. A circle of red-bereted Oketz handlers, their heads bowed, their eyes welling up with tears, surrounded the grave. With their dogs at their sides, they all gave Toshi the tribute he deserved. Caleb, who attended with Liat, wanted to bark out his farewell to his friend, but was unable to do so because of the muzzles that the dogs were required to wear at these times in order to maintain the respectful silence.

"Walk softly since here is the resting place of Israeli soldiers," Lt. Col. Barak reminded everyone as he concluded the service. "Toshi was one of us," he said in a sad, shaky voice. "We have lost one of our brothers in arms."

The years flew by with Caleb fulfilling his duties as an Oketz dog. After many brave and outstanding performances, he too was awarded a medal of honor. The time came, however, for his military career to end; after seven years he was considered a "veteran" ready for retirement.

For Oketz dogs retirement could mean several things. Some went home with their handlers, but this was not possible for Caleb. Liat was getting married and her husband was allergic to dogs. Some dogs became guard dogs on Israeli Air Force bases. Caleb was to embark on a different adventure.

CHAPTER SIX

"Yes," Rabbi Tracht repeated himself. "I suspect that Caleb has a very interesting story."

"Bo," the Rabbi said to Caleb. Caleb walked toward the Rabbi. "Shev," the Rabbi continued to command. Caleb sat. "Kelev tov," the Rabbi said as he patted Caleb on this head. The Rabbi smiled as he looked up at Captain Dart.

"What did you say to him?" the Dart asked.

"I told him to come and sit; when he responded to my commands, I told him that he was a good dog. My commands were in Hebrew."

"Hebrew?" Officer Dart questioned. "Why would Caleb know Hebrew?"

"Were you here when Caleb first arrived in Helena?" asked the Rabbi.

"No, I was transferred here later when the officer whose place I took died."

"You were never given information about where the dog came from?"

"No, I was just told that he was imported from somewhere and that he was an outstanding bomb-sniffing dog. The officer whom I replaced left no records of his background."

"Well, this is what I believe is Caleb's story", the Rabbi began. "Like many other Belgian Malinois dogs, he was probably a member of the Israel Defense Forces K-9 Special Forces Unit called Oketz. He and his handler probably accompanied other units on secret missions. Since you say that you know Caleb is a bomb sniffer, which would have been his mission. These are very brave, very special dogs. My son Yossi was a handler of a dog named Toshi, who died in action. I attended the dog's funeral, a very solemn, respectful affair where these dogs are honored for their loyalty and sacrifice. Yes, I suspect that you have a very special dog here. If you would like, I can give you some help. You will have to learn some Hebrew."

"You think I can learn?" Captain Dart asked, doubtfully.

"I think you can," encouraged Rabbi Tracht. Some sounds like the "<u>ch</u>" sound may be difficult for you, but I think you can do it."

In the days that followed, Captain Dart worked hard with Rabbi Tracht to learn Hebrew. More command words, such as "ragly" (heel), "artza" (down), "amod" (stand), and, of course Caleb's beloved "ta'vi" (fetch or retrieve) became part of Captain Dart's daily vocabulary. As he learned more and more, his relationship with Caleb improved. Caleb became very protective of the captain, just as he had been with Liat. Their bond became very strong. And Caleb became the best bomb-sniffing dog in all of Montana!

One day, as Captain Dart was cleaning out an old, never-used cabinet, he came across some papers that revealed how Caleb had come to Montana. The Helena police department had needed a bomb-sniffing dog but didn't have the $20,000 to buy one. Instead, they discovered that they could get such a dog from the IDF in Israel for just the price of a plane ticket! This was right at the time when Caleb's IDF career was coming to an end, and he was available.

So Caleb took the second plane ride of his life. This time, when he arrived in the cool, clear air of Montana, there was no red-bereted pretty soldier waiting for him, smiling and saying "Shalom, Caleb. Welcome to Oketz." Instead there was a black-capped policeman, with a shiny badge, uttering words that Caleb could not understand and taking him to places that he could not recognize. But that would change.

And, slowly but surely, it did.

ABOUT THE AUTHOR

Cynthia Goren cherishes her role as a Jewish grandmother. Having taught both children and adults, she has devoted herself to the continuity of the Jewish people by telling their story to her children, grandchildren, and all those who will listen.

She lives with her husband in suburban Chicago (near their grandchildren).

18553798R00048

Made in the USA
Lexington, KY
12 November 2012